Santa is coming to Wisconsin

Written by Steve Smallman

Illustrated by Robert Dunn and Katherine Kirkland

sourcebooks
jabberwocky

"Well?"

boomed Santa. "Have all the children from **Wisconsin** been good this year?"

"Well...uh...mostly," answered the little old elf, as he bustled across the busy workshop to Santa's desk.

Santa peered down at the elf from behind the tall, teetering piles of letters that the children of Wisconsin had sent him.

"Mostly?" asked Santa,
looking over the top of his glasses.

"Yes...but they've all been **especially** good in the last few days!" said the elf.

Santa is coming to Wisconsin

Written by Steve Smallman
Illustrated by Robert Dunn and Katherine Kirkland
Designed by Sarah Allen

Copyright © Hometown World Ltd. 2012

Published by Sourcebooks Jabberwocky, an imprint of Sourcebooks, Inc.
P.O. Box 4410, Naperville, Illinois 60567-4410
(630) 961-3900
Fax: (630) 961-2168
www.jabberwockykids.com

Library of Congress Cataloging-in-Publication data is on file with the publisher.

Source of Production: Leo Paper Products, Guangdong Province, China
Date of Production: May 2013
Run Number: HTW-PO010313
Printed and bound in China
LEO 10 9 8 7 6 5 4 3 2

"Jolly good!" chuckled Santa.
"Then we'd better get their presents loaded up!"

Even though the sack of presents was

really, really big

and the elves were really, really small,

they seemed to have no trouble loading it onto Santa's sleigh.
Though how they managed to fit such a big sack onto one little sleigh
even they didn't know. But somehow they did.

"Splendid!" boomed Santa. "We're ready to go!"

"Er...not quite, Santa," said the little old elf. "One of our reindeer is missing!"

"Missing?

Which reindeer is missing?" asked Santa.

"The youngest one, Santa," said the elf. "It's his first flight tonight. I've called him and called him, but..."

Just then, a young reindeer strolled up, munching on a large carrot.

"Where have you been?"

asked Santa.

The youngest reindeer was crunching so loudly that it was no wonder he hadn't heard the little old elf calling.

"Oh well, never mind," said Santa, giving the reindeer a little wink. He took out his Santa-nav and tapped in the coordinates for Wisconsin. "This will guide us to Wisconsin in no time."

Crunch!
Crunch!
Crunch!

With a flick of the reins and a jerk of the harness, off they went, racing through the sky.

"Ho, ho, ho!"
laughed Santa.

"We'll soon have these presents delivered to the Badger State!"

Santa's sleigh flew through the starry night heading south across the Arctic Ocean. On they flew in the crisp, wintry air, crossing over Canada. In the wink of an eye, the sleigh was flying above Minnesota and on to Wisconsin. The youngest reindeer was very excited. He had never been away from the North Pole before.

They had just crossed Lake Superior
when, suddenly, they ran into a blizzard.
Snowflakes whirled around the sleigh.

They couldn't see a thing!

The youngest reindeer was getting a bit worried,
but Santa didn't seem concerned.

"In two miles…"

said the Santa-nav in a bossy lady's voice,

"…keep left at the next star."

"But, ma'am," Santa blustered, "I can't see any stars in all this snow!"
Soon they were

hopelessly lost!

Ding-dong!
Ding-dong!

Then, through the howling blizzard, the youngest reindeer heard a faint ringing sound.

Ding-dong!

He looked over at the old reindeer with the red nose. But he had his head down.

(Red nose...I wonder who that could be?!)

Ding-dong!
Ding-dong!

Ding-dong! Ding-dong!

There was that sound again, like church bells ringing. The youngest reindeer turned around to look at Santa. But Santa wasn't listening. He seemed to be arguing with a little box with buttons on it.

With a flick of the harness and a jerk of the reins, the youngest reindeer gave a sharp *tug* and headed off toward the sound of the bells, pulling Santa and his sleigh behind him!

"Whoa!"

cried Santa, pulling his hat straight. "What's going on?" Then, to his surprise, he heard the ringing sound.

"Well done, young reindeer!" he shouted cheerfully. "It must be the bells of the Cathedral of St. John the Evangelist. Don't worry, children, Santa is coming!"

Then, suddenly...

CRUNCH!

The sleigh hit something as it plummeted through the snow clouds. **"You have arrived!"** said the Santa-nav unhelpfully.

Finally, when the snow had died down and the clouds parted, Santa discovered exactly where they were...

...stuck, right at the very top of **Milwaukee City Hall!**

"Everybody, PULL!"

The reindeer *pulled* with all their might until, at last, with a screeching noise, the sleigh scraped clear of the tower and Santa steered them safely over East Town, above Yankee Hill, past the North Point Water Tower, and down into Lakeshore State Park.

Luckily, there
was no real
damage done, but
the packages had all
been jumbled up. Santa
quickly sorted the presents
into order again.

"All right," said Santa. "Thanks
to this young reindeer I know where
we are now. Don't worry, children,

Santa is coming!"

Santa drove his sleigh expertly from rooftop to rooftop all over Wisconsin, popping in and out of chimneys as fast as he could go.

(Which was pretty fast for a chubby fellow!)

There were big chimneys in Madison, and small chimneys in Appleton. He squeezed down thin chimneys in Racine, and plummeted down fat chimneys in Oshkosh.

The youngest reindeer was amazed at how quickly they went. Santa never seemed to get tired at all! And it looked like the children in Wisconsin were going to be very lucky this year! But the youngest reindeer was starting to feel a bit weary and quite hungry too!

He piled them under the Christmas trees and carefully filled up the stockings with surprises.

In house after house, Santa delved inside his sack for packages of every shape and size.

Santa took a little bite out of each cookie,
a tiny sip of milk, wiped his beard, and
popped the carrots into his sack.

In house after house, the good children of
Wisconsin had left out a plate of cookies,
a small glass of milk, and a big,
crunchy carrot.

From Kenosha to Green Bay, from
Eau Claire to Waupaca, from La Crosse to
the Dells, and ALL the places in between,
Santa and his sleigh visited every house
in Wisconsin.

Santa delivered presents to Andrew, Alison, Anna, Arabella, Archie, Ashley... the list went on and on! ...Zac, Zara, Zeb, Zoe, Zybil. ←

(Zybil? That must be a spelling mistake, surely!)

Finally, Santa had delivered the last present on his long Wisconsin list.

"Great moons and stars!" sighed Santa. "It's past midnight and my sack seems as heavy as ever! I hope I haven't forgotten anyone."

Santa opened his sack to check...but it was full of juicy, crunchy carrots!

Santa divided the carrots among all the reindeer.
"Well done!" he said, patting the youngest reindeer gently on the nose.

But the youngest reindeer didn't hear him...he was too busy munching!

Then it was time to set off for home. Santa reset his Santa-nav for
the North Pole, and soon they were speeding above Madison, past the
Wisconsin State Capitol, and past Lake Monona, through the crisp, starry night.

"Ho, ho, ho!"
laughed Santa.

"Merry Christmas, Wisconsin!"